Sierra Becomes a Search Dog

by Robert D. Calkins

Illustrated by Taillefer Long

Sniff
Sniff

Sniff Sniff

Sniff
Sniff

Sniff
Sniff

SIERRA BECOMES A SEARCH DOG
by Robert D. Calkins

CALLOUT PRESS
Olalla, Washington
SierraSearchDog.com
RobertDCalkins.com

Illustrations and Design by Taillefer Long
info@IlluminatedStories.com

ISBN: 978-0-9971911-0-3
Library of Congress Control Number: 2016901164

Dedicated to Sierra.

I asked you to sniff for people,
and you reminded me to stop and smell the flowers.

Sierra Becomes a Search Dog

by Robert D. Calkins

Illustrated by Taillefer Long

Once there was a little Golden Retriever puppy named Sierra.

Sierra was very curious.
She sniffed everything.

Sniff
Sniff

She sniffed the shoe....

She sniffed the socks...

Sniff

Sniff

She sniffed the flowers,...

She sniffed the box!

Sierra even helped Bryce
play hide-and-seek.

She used her nose to sniff out
where everyone had hidden.

When she found someone,
she gave them lots of puppy kisses.
Sierra loved playing hide-and-seek.

FUN FACTS

Did you know that, to a dog,
every person smells different?

Bryce's father had an idea.
"Maybe Sierra could be a Search and Rescue dog," he thought.

Sierra was so good at hide-and-seek,
she could certainly find people who were lost in the woods.

Sierra and Bryce spent lots of time practicing,
and Sierra became a very good search dog.

Whenever Sierra would find people,
she would be rewarded with her favorite ball!

Sierra liked searching so much that she would sniff someone's hat or coat . . .

. . . and then go find them.

Even when they didn't really
want to be found!

One day the neighbors came over looking for their little girl, Betty. She'd been gone a long time.

"We think she's in the woods. She wasn't supposed to go there by herself. She may be lost!"

They knew how good Sierra was at hide-and-seek, so they asked if Sierra might be able to find their daughter.

"Do you think Sierra can help us?"

Bryce let Sierra sniff Betty's sweater to learn her scent.
They went quickly to the woods.

Just like in practice,
Sierra started sniffing the ground.

Sierra sniffed by the big tree.

Sniff Sniff

She sniffed by
the small bush.

She went down the trail
with everyone right behind.

They went a long way down the trail. Sierra had to search for a long time but stuck with it and never gave up. Finally, behind a tree, there was Betty!

"I went out on the trail and must have gone the wrong way," Betty said.

Her parents were very happy that Betty was OK and she got lots of puppy kisses.

Bryce told Sierra, "We've practiced and practiced,
but now you've done it for real.

"Sierra, you're officially a Search and Rescue dog."

FUN FACTS

What makes a good search dog?
A SAR dog needs a very good nose, but also needs
to be strong, be big enough to push through heavy
brush, and be able to walk in the woods for hours.

About the Author

Robert "Bob" Calkins has been a search and rescue dog handler in Kitsap County, Washington, for more than a dozen years. Bob currently searches with K9 Ruger, a four-year old Golden Retriever who passed his SAR test in the spring of 2015. He and his dogs have responded to everything from routine missing person cases, to homicides, to the horrific landslide that in 2014 swept over homes in the tiny community of Oso, Washington.

Bob is the author of the **SIERRA THE SEARCH DOG** series of books for children and adults.

About the Real Sierra

Sierra was Bob's first search dog, a Golden Retriever with the well-known "Golden smile" and a natural ability to find people who'd gotten lost. She liked nothing better than running through the woods hoping to pick up the scent of a missing person. Her paycheck was a simple tennis ball, and a scratch on the head. She worked with Bob for five years, responding to many missing person searches in and around western Washington.

About the Illustrator

Taillefer Long is an illustrator and designer based in Charleston, SC. He loves visual storytelling, the creative process, and seeing ideas come to life. Taillefer has collaborated with many authors, illustrating and designing books for over a decade. His childhood Basset Hound, Aesop, was an expert cuddler and drooler but could have used a little obedience training from Bob!

Taillefer's work can be found at IlluminatedStories.com and DancingInkArt.com.